THE BIG BAD BOOK OF BEDTIME STORIES

VOLUME 1

The Big Bad Book of Bedtime Stories

RYLEY BANKS

Published by Three Lemon Press, LLC

ISBN: 978-1-962835-09-1 (ebook) 978-1-962835-10-7 (paperback)

Cover Design: Leslie Noyes, Leslie Noyes Creative Consulting

Cover Image: Vikingur on DepositPhotos

Sensitivity Reader for *Third Time's the Charm*: Tobias Kashman

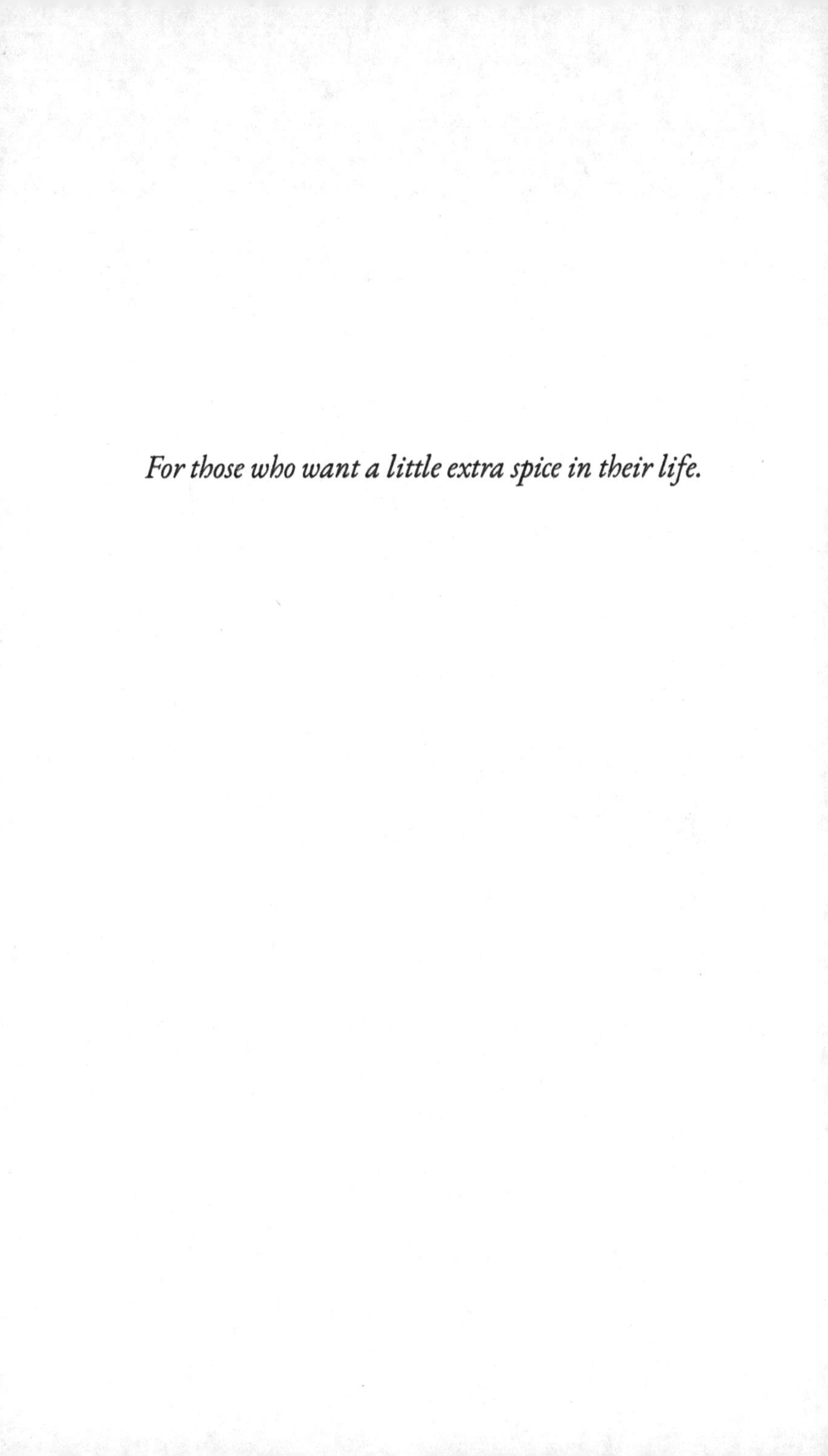

For those who want a little extra spice in their life.

Content Advisory

Content advisories for all of Ryley's books are available here: https://ryleybanks.com/books/contentwarnings/

There are two ways you can use this section:
1) As a list of things to avoid;
OR
2) As a menu of things to look forward to.

I trust you to know yourself. Happy reading either way.

xoxo Ryley

EGGPLANT NIGHT

Jax and Bree have a weekly date night, marked with a certain emoji on their shared calendar. They've done a lot as a couple—axe throwing, cooking classes, outdoor concerts—but tonight is different. After they shared their most taboo desires, this date night is a group activity.

Pairing: MF main couple, but the story is FMMMM+

Tropes: married couple / established couple, fantasy fulfillment, spicy date night, all about her, hotwife, free use, BDSM (light bondage)

Eggplant Night

"Bree?"

Jax stroked a hand down the back of my head, raking through my wavy, dark hair until my spine was liquid. After not nearly long enough, he placed a mug down in front of me and sat in his spot across the oak kitchen table with a steaming mug of his own. Then he blushed and began to shred a napkin. I cocked an eyebrow. Whatever it was, this was going to be good.

Since he so clearly needed a moment to gather his thoughts, I took a swig of hot coffee and finished typing an appointment in my phone's calendar app, eyes flicking to our weekly Friday night date. I'd started marking it with an eggplant emoji years ago, and I smiled at the silly—and sexy—reminder. Then I put my phone down to give him, and the coffee, my full attention.

"What's on your mind?" I scooted forward and met his gaze.

"Remember...remember our conversation a few months ago?"

Did I *ever*. Prompted by a friend's shocking affair, we'd spent an entire evening, and more wine than I cared to admit, confessing our deepest fantasies to each other. Even though we'd been married a decade, apparently we hadn't even scratched the surface—but when you bind yourself to someone for *forever*, no one outright tells you that neither of you are mind-readers and you need to talk about that shit.

"Uh huh," I said neutrally and sipped my drink. I watched him under my downcast eyelashes as he psyched himself up to continue. If possible, he was even more handsome than when we first got together. Fuck our twenties. Mid-thirties looked better and better.

An email notification chirped on my phone; I silenced it and tossed it onto the third chair. Jax would always come first.

"Would you be up for doing something a little different for date night this week?" he asked.

We'd done everything from the classic dinner-and-a-movie to escape rooms and axe throwing. "Sure. Have something in mind?"

Jax met my eyes over his coffee cup. "When you went for your physical last month, did they send you a copy of your STI test?"

Huh?

If his goal was to keep me off-balance, he was knocking it out of the park. "Yeah. All negative, of course." I tilted my head, curiosity officially piqued. "Jax, what's this—"

"Bree—were you serious about doing some of what we discussed?"

My mouth went dry, the list replaying in my mind in all its taboo glory. Nothing we'd talked about that evening was off-limits, at least with some serious discussion first. But *some* fantasies...

Game on.

I took his hand and squeezed. "Only if it's together. And safe."

"Good. I was hoping we were still on the same page," he said. "Because I might—*might*—have found a way to make one of yours—and mine—come true."

"What?" My heart thundered so hard I was afraid it would crack my ribs open. "Which one?" Anticipation of the unknown racked me with shivers.

Jax shook his head. "Nothing's final. But..." He got up and pulled an unassuming manila folder off the counter and set it in front of me. The chair creaked as he sat again. "I needed to make sure you were fully on board."

Jax opened the folder and tapped a blank line next to one he'd already signed. "Your signature." He licked his lips. "Do you trust me?"

He was earnest, honest, and, most importantly, mine.

My answer came as easy as breathing. "With my life."

With how quickly I moved the pen, I was surprised my signature didn't catch the paper on fire.

Some husbands surprised their wives with flowers.

Some husbands surprised their wives with chocolate.

Some husbands, apparently, surprised their wives with a night of exploring their deepest fantasies together.

Fuck, am I lucky.

———

ALL WEEK, Jax refused to give me any details of our Friday eggplant night.

I even played dirty with a drawn-out blow job. Cock leaking on my tongue, I licked the rosy crown like a lollipop, bringing him to the brink over and over before I firmly grabbed the base of his dick with my thumb and forefinger and asked him what our plans were.

Dark eyes taunted and pleaded, but I held him there, throbbing and steel-hard, cherry red and dripping pearly drops of precum. And still he refused to give in.

It was either an iron will, or a bigger desire to see me in as much ecstasy later in the week.

Finally I let him come, one hand in my yoga pants circling my throbbing clit as I pumped him. He spurted on my breasts and I milked him through it, streams of cum running over my hand until he began to soften.

Jax's blinding smile melted my insides when he guided me to my feet and then knelt before me. "Sweetheart, if you really want to know, I'll tell you. Just ask me again."

I didn't.

But that could also be because, in an instant, my pants were down to my knees, my clit in his mouth, and the only words I knew were "yes" and his name.

———

With each passing day, the squirmy caterpillars in my stomach grew to full-on butterflies. I'd never experienced anything like this anticipation, not even for our wedding. What fantasy were we fulfilling? Where were we going? Would anyone else be there?

In the spirit of the surprise Jax had planned, I even refused to search online for a place in our city that would cater to whatever it was we were doing, unwilling to ruin it for myself. I didn't know where to start anyway—sex toy shop? BDSM club? Local bookstore with an exceptionally curated smut section?

The only indication I had all day Friday that anything was different from a normal eggplant night was a series of texts from Jax making sure I was taking good care of myself until he could.

After I got home and took a shower, a comfortable yet sexy outfit was laid out for me on the bed, black lacy underwear I'd never seen before right next to it. The bra pushed my breasts up, hard nipples straining through the sheer lace. The cute hip huggers made my ass look fabulous, the material soft and sensuous over my skin.

"I *will* say, you won't be in it long. But I thought you'd like to feel extra gorgeous tonight."

I turned at Jax's voice, heart in my throat. He stood in the doorway, freshly showered and casually dressed in dark jeans and a button-down shirt, sleeves rolled to the elbows. Something about the exposed forearm, as Victorian as it sounded, always made me bite my lip. Probably because I imagined the muscles flexing there, the veins standing out as he'd drive his long fingers into my pussy, striving to please me.

"Thank you," I said, smoothing my hands down my front. "They're beautiful." Then, I innocently added, "What do you mean I won't be wearing them long?"

Jax laughed, the sound of his chuckle deep and full. "C'mon. We don't want to be late."

After I put on my clothes—a flowing skirt and low, scoop-necked tank paired with strappy sandals—we headed out. Jax had thought of everything, hailing a ride that was already waiting at the curb. It took us downtown and let us off at a corner in an area populated with older brick buildings. From there, we walked a block to a whitewashed edifice. There was no sign on the exterior, but Jax laced our fingers together and led me to an unlocked side door. Once inside a small foyer—with two security cameras—he spoke into an intercom to verify our reservation, and we were officially buzzed through another door and into the building.

Goosebumps spread over my skin as we followed signs guiding us to a dim but comfortable waiting room. Big leather couches, richly dyed in a cognac brown, dominated the space, walls covered in deep emerald damask patterns. Jax and I were the only ones there.

"So, any guesses? I *know* you've been thinking about it all week." Jax nosed my neck, running his lips along the tense tendon before giving it a sharp nip. My whole body ignited. He soothed the bite with his tongue.

His vibe had changed as soon as we'd been allowed in —gone was the blushing, shy man who'd had trouble asking if I wanted to do this, replaced by a guy with serious big dick energy.

"None," I said. I wound my arms around his waist, clutching him close. Already, his cock pressed against my abdomen. There was something comforting about his arousal, and it helped quell doubts that he wanted this—whatever *this* was—even though he'd only expressed worry the past week about whether *I* was all in. "Didn't have a clue where to begin."

"Fair enough. Let's start with what fantasy you think we're here for."

I pulled back just enough to see his dancing eyes. "Hmm. Something with equipment or toys we...don't have at home?"

"On the right track." Jax slid a hand over the outside of my tank. One finger traced along the deep neckline, dipping underneath to the lacy cup of my bra. Our lips met as he taunted the nipple hiding there—a direct line to all my pleasure centers—and my clit begged him to trail his hand southward.

"What, nothing?" Jax said. "Cat got your tongue?"

"Maybe if you give me a hint?" I pouted, wrapping my fingers around him through his pants. Fuck, I needed him inside me.

"Well, since you asked so nicely..." He gave me another kiss, this one sweeter than the last, and led me to one of the couches.

We sat and he moved in, so close we pressed together from hip to shoulder, and whispered, "I'm not sure you even remember saying this, but...we're here tonight to...what did you tell me you wanted? To be fucked by a whole group of guys, their only goal to fill your sweet little hole up with cum?"

My jaw dropped as I thought back to that night. I'd had a few glasses of wine, but, beyond the haze of lowered inhibitions, I recalled telling Jax I wanted exactly that.

I *heard*, rather than felt, the blood rush through my body as I flushed from head to cunt. Everything went tight and wet, readying for the penetration that was coming.

His lips moved at my ear, breath warm. "I'll ask you again. Is this something you want? Because we don't have to do this, tonight or any other time—"

"Yes," I said. "As long as our rules are in place."

Jax beamed. "Absolutely." He kissed my temple. "I've wanted to give you this, but, you know, it's a little difficult for just *me* to..." He gestured to my lower half.

"Jax—you're more than enough for me. Always. And thank you." I drew him into a soft kiss.

"Jax and Bree?" A well-dressed woman, probably in her early twenties, entered the room. Now that I knew what the night would hold, I couldn't help the tremor that shot through my body as we got up and walked over to her. She smiled.

"I'm Chloe," she said, and tapped a clipboard. "Bree, your husband has made all the arrangements and mentioned this would be a surprise for you. Read these and sign, please." She handed over a form detailing the experience, different paperwork from what Jax had had me sign before.

"Excellent," Chloe said when we were done. "I'll show you to your changing room."

As we left the waiting area, I said, "You're the first person we've seen. Are we your only clients tonight?"

Chloe laughed. "Oh, no. Far from it. We're almost always fully booked on Fridays. Lots of people want to let off steam from the work week. But discretion is our business, and we're very good at it. Tonight I, and the phalanx, will be the only people you'll interact with."

"Phalanx?" I asked.

"Our team of male escorts," Chloe explained. "They're very...talented."

She led us through a maze of doors and hallways. The building was surprisingly quiet—there were no noises to indicate anything was going on, or even that anyone else was there.

Chloe gestured to a numbered door with a key in the lock. "You'll remove your clothes, put on the robes provided, then lock your door on the way out. Keep your key in your robe pocket. You'll be able to hang it up in the playroom. Come out into the hall when you're ready."

Playroom. Phalanx. My mind whirred and I went giddy, still unable to picture what this night would really look like.

Jax pulled open the heavy wooden door, and I followed him in. The changing room was spacious, more of a suite. It was furnished with a loveseat and table, and the adjoining shower and bathroom were well-appointed with luxury toiletries. I slowly stripped for my husband, showing off the lacy lingerie, Jax's eyes lighting my skin up the whole time.

Standing in front of the full-length mirror without a stitch on, I expected to feel more...exposed. Nervous. But instead, I was excited, elated. I blew out a deep breath. How lucky was I to be with someone who was willing to indulge me in something so taboo?

Jax, already naked, came up behind me and helped me into a robe. The satiny fabric melted luxuriously against my skin. Before I could belt it, Jax slid a finger through the slippery sheen between my lower lips.

"Mmm. You're so ready for this, aren't you. Ready to be a good little toy for me? For all of them?"

I groaned and ground myself against his finger, which he took away with a wicked grin. My body missed what it hadn't even had yet. How cruel.

"This way," Chloe said, when we finally emerged. My toes gripped the plush carpeting as we walked, the satin robe slithering around my skin like the snake seducing Eve. We stopped at the far end of the hall in front of an imposing door. "Your fantasy is inside this room. Please hang your robes on the hooks. Liam will guide your experience, and he'll be in shortly."

The door and lock clicked securely behind us, the sound practically echoing in the quiet space.

Alone with my husband, I hesitated for a moment before Jax took my robe and hung it next to his. I looked around, getting my bearings. The playroom was warmly lit and comfortable, with sensual, dark fabric against the walls.

The only piece of furniture sat squarely in the middle of the room. Low and similar in shape to a pommel horse, it was domed like a half-moon. The padding, covered in spotless, deep red leather, looked perfect for cushioning hips, or even an entire torso if used lengthwise. It was supported by sturdy metal legs that extended out to distribute the weight and prevent it from tipping over. I knelt next to it to see what was attached—soft, adjustable leather cuffs, tethered by a short length of chain. Four of them. My breath hitched as I realized someone could be bent over and bound to it.

No, not someone.

Me.

I could be bound that way.

To that—

"Do you like the breeding bench?"

I started at the smooth male voice and looked up. A handsome—and very naked—man approached from a hidden door opposite where Jax and I had entered. His body seemed to ripple as he moved closer.

"Sorry to startle you. I'm Liam."

I stood, unsure of whether I should shake his hand or drop to my knees when he'd shortly be plowing me into next Tuesday. I giggled a little hysterically. "Bree," I said on an exhale.

"Jax," my husband said. "Nice to finally meet you in person." At my questioning look, he motioned to Liam. "We planned this together."

"Bree." My name on Liam's lips was a statement. A command. With that one word, he had my full attention, and I was ready to comply. It wasn't often that I surprised myself, but the feeling of simply letting go was just so...easy. "Brace yourself on one end of the bench. We're going to prepare you."

I scrambled to obey, turning around and bending at the waist. The cool leather wrinkled a little under my fingertips. Liam crouched in front of me, between me and the—I shivered, just thinking *breeding bench*. He firmly tapped the insides of my thighs with a hand, and I automatically spread them more.

"Good girl," he said. A part of me I'd long ignored preened at the praise.

The next thing I knew, a warm hand was on my upper back between my shoulder blades, pressing me down further. The hand pet my hair. Jax. Even the gentle reminder he was there, experiencing this *with* me, was enough to calm any lingering anxiety.

Jax's cool, lubed cock touched my heated core, and I gasped as it filled me with quick, yet gentle, thrusts. I'd know the feel and shape of Jax's cock anywhere. The defined ridge of his crown, the thick girth toward the root. He slid in, sweet as anything, and somewhere in the depths of my mind I realized he was hotter and harder than I'd ever felt him before. Maybe because we had an audience—the man who'd be fucking me next.

I glanced down when I realized I'd forgotten he was there. In front of and below me, Liam met my eyes, a mischievous grin on his lush mouth.

"What are we..." I started, but Jax's hips made contact with my ass, and suddenly speaking was the furthest thing from my mind.

"...doing?" Liam finished. "Well, *your* tight little cunt is going to get nice and wet while your husband fucks you, and *I'm* going to eat your pussy. Would you like that?"

"Ye—yes!"

Jax snapped his hips forward and I tilted my pelvis, eager for more. But his rhythm, his thrusts, it was all—different. No slow drags along my quivering walls; no grinding, full pumps. Quick and fast and dirty. Not even a fuck—just a hard-core rut.

As he'd promised, I was a toy, a device, for getting off.

A receptacle for his cum.

Exactly.

What.

I'd.

Fucking.

Wanted.

Then Liam grabbed my hips, braced me against Jax's onslaught, and pressed his mouth against my heated flesh, teasing my lips apart with his tongue. My clit ached when he traced it and I tried to grind forward into his talented mouth, chasing the high of fucking into him and being fucked from behind.

Over the sharp slap of skin-on-skin, I heard a soft sound and my eyes roved upward. With each quick thrust, it seemed like a new man appeared in front of me, circling around the breeding bench, eyes greedy and cocks stiff, watching me get fucked, knowing they were going to be doing the same. That they'd get their turn. My walls clenched around Jax's cock in antic-ipation.

I howled as Jax grunted, his wet cock flying in and out of me, and it wasn't long after that he pushed forward, shoving me hard against Liam's mouth, and I came, grabbing Liam's curls with one hand, grinding into his face. Jax twitched inside of me, his cock spurting deep in my cunt.

"You take me so well, sweetheart, and you'll take them all just as perfectly," Jax whispered in my ear. "I wanted to be the first tonight to fill you up. And maybe I'll have you again before we're through."

He pulled out, keeping me bent over with a gentle hand on my back. Liam scooted around the side, gesturing me to move up a step or two. I hobbled forward on shaky legs, still trembling with aftershocks, and allowed him to bind my ankles to the bench. I leaned parallel over one of the short ends of the bench, almost straddling it, my breasts pressed against the surface. If I went on tiptoe, I could either arch my back or grind my clit against the soft leather.

"I'm not going to bind your hands," Liam told me. "We want you to be able to move and brace yourself. Touch yourself, even." He stood, cock hard and thick between his legs, and circled back behind me.

Surprisingly, Jax sat by the side of the breeding bench

on a small chair that appeared out of nowhere and took one of my hands. "Ready?" he asked with a grin.

I didn't even get a chance to answer before Liam gently touched my opening, swiping his finger through Jax's leaking cum. I turned—the ankle bindings kept my legs separated, but I had a good range of motion—and groaned when he spread the wetness over his own cock.

Movement behind Liam caught my eye, too—the men, all naked, fit, and hard, had formed a line. All for me. In a matter of minutes, I'd be filled with their cocks and load after load of cream. I couldn't fucking wait.

I turned to face forward, meeting Jax's eyes just as Liam pushed in. His cock had an upward curve, the fat head eagerly parting my walls. My mouth dropped open, and I couldn't stop the moan from spilling out as he ravaged me. His hips pounded against my ass with no regard for my pleasure, but the act of him simply *taking* made me sopping wet. My nipples pebbled where they rubbed against the smooth leather and I grunted, tipping my hips to take him deeper. His fingers dug into my sides, keeping me positioned exactly where he wanted me, a good little cock slut. All too soon his rhythm stuttered, cock throbbing with each hot pulse of cum before he pulled out with a wet slide.

The scent of cum and my own musky arousal hung heavy in the air.

Without warning, I was immediately filled again. This man's dick was shorter—when he bottomed out, pelvis touching my ass, he wasn't uncomfortably deep —and slimmer. He ran a hand up my spine to the back of my neck and, with a firm "Stay down," pressed me to the bench. The friction from his vigorous thrusting stimulated my sensitive opening in the best way. I arched my back, on tiptoe as high as I could be, determined to be the perfect little hole.

"Oh, Bree," Jax said, squeezing my hand. "You like that new cock? Look at you take him. He can't get enough."

I turned my head, cheek against the leather, gazing at Jax where he sat next to me. He was flushed and his breath came in ragged pants, mouth pouty and open in a mirror of mine, his other hand on his dick. Up until then, there'd still been a part of me that hadn't completely bought that this was something Jax wanted as well. And knowing he was getting as much out of this as I was...

Set.

Me.

On.

Fire.

I clenched around the cock fucking me, encouraging the man to use me like a toy. His hands slid under my chest and long fingers plucked my nipples on their way down to my hips to hold me still. With no room to move between us, he flooded my cunt with warm cum, and I climaxed all over his cock, yelling Jax's name.

Before I even came down from that high, another blunt, hot cockhead rubbed my lower lips, coating himself with my wetness and the cum leaking from my hole. Slowly, the new man pressed in. Instinctively I shoved back, eager to sheathe him, to take him inside. But I was so full, so well-used, that cum streamed out around him, sliding down my thighs.

"Bree, you're doing so good, but he's so goddamn big, gotta go slow, don't want to hurt you." Jax reached over and stroked my cheek and over my bottom lip. I licked the pad of his thumb and allowed him inside my mouth, his skin salty. "Sweetheart, you need something to suck on, don't you? So good for me."

The guy behind me worked his way inside, the loads I'd already taken slicking the way, his defined head rutting through any resistance. He was thick, oh, so fucking thick. I breathed through it, relaxing to accommodate his girth. Soon, his balls pressed against my ass cheeks, full and heavy and ready to fill me. He didn't fuck so much as *grind*, hips flush with my ass and swiveling them so every inch of me was stretched. He lowered himself, chest against my back, grunting savagely, taking taking *taking*, until that big dick pulsed, shooting his release inside me.

"Wait!" I cried out, reaching back with the hand that wasn't holding Jax's to grab the guy's thigh before he pulled away. He must have known what I wanted because he stayed seated inside me, keeping me so, so stretched, even though he was softening, letting me grind against the breeding bench, slip-sliding to rub my clit until I screamed again, walls squeezing around him as my world and body detonated.

"That's it, Bree," Jax whispered. "Keep taking them—I want you so full of their cum. I want you covered in it because you can't hold it all."

As time went on, I didn't even look back. Didn't want to, didn't care. True to my fantasy, their only goal was to fuck and pump me full. I was theirs for the taking, a sloppy wet hole to fill. And I loved every minute of it.

I lost track of the men who took me and the number of times I came, wailing my pleasure into the sound-proofed room. But the one thing that kept me grounded, the one thing I was aware of, was that one hand was always in Jax's. His eyes were dark with arousal, pupils eating up the iris. Hungry for me. Hungry for me to have *this*.

The last man pulled out, my body both empty and filled to the brim. I struggled to catch my breath as my husband moved to the space behind me again. I lifted my ass, presenting, showing him how full I was. How wet I was between my legs. How good I'd been.

"Look at you," he said, running a finger through the stream of cream running from my body and down my legs. "So beautiful. And mine. All mine..." His voice trailed off as he rubbed his dick, rock hard again, against my tender folds and through the dripping mess.

My body clenched around nothing, aching for Jax to *take*.

But he didn't.

Instead, he slid his crown up and down my cleft, circling my swollen clit, and back to my opening. Running his length through the wetness, slow and tender. Sometimes he'd dip the throbbing, hot head in, just for a few shallow thrusts, then pull back out to do it all again. He took himself in hand, jerking off with his cockhead pressed against my body, rubbing it up and down my lower lips. The obscene slick sound of his hand as he stroked made me cry out, eager for one last load. Finally, warm streaks covered my pussy as he groaned and came, marking me up on the outside. My orgasm spread through me like honey.

I collapsed, sated and full, against the red leather bench. Jax immediately undid the ankle cuffs, rubbing the skin where I'd been fixed in place. He kissed the small of my back, resting his cheek against me for a moment before lifting me up off the breeding bench. When I stood, wobbly, I was surprised we were the only two people in the room.

Still floating on an incredible high, Jax had to help me into my robe before he put his on. Chloe returned to take us back to our changing room, making it clear we could take as long as we wanted to be together in the suite.

Exhaustion hit and I settled on the loveseat. Jax took my robe off and cleaned me up, gently wiping with a warm, soft cloth until every sticky drop was gone.

"Was it everything you hoped for?" he asked, curled up against me and stroking my hair. We'd definitely be taking advantage of the shower, but for now, this was perfect.

"More than." I stretched, feeling a pleasant ache in my legs. "But the best part was that you were there with me."

Jax kissed my forehead. "For me, too. I hope the next one is just as fun."

Then he held me close on the sofa and whispered sweet nothings as we slipped into sleep, the perfect end to a fantasy evening.

Until our next eggplant night.

DIRTY DISHES

I should be ashamed when my wife invites him over to take care of my chores. She's going to get very dirty—with him. I'll be there to clean her up when she's ready. But first, she requires I do the dishes like a good boy.

Pairing: MFM

Tropes: hotwife, cuckold, shame and humiliation kink, married couple / established couple, acts of service, consensual power dynamics

DIRTY DISHES

Her voice carries over the kitchen faucet, moans mixing with the wet rush of the water as the stainless sink fills. I want nothing more than to drive into her slick heat, fuck her over the edge—but I can't. Tonight, *he* gets her first.

And, just like every time we play, I have a job to do.

As soon as she got home earlier, she leaned back against the door, hands clasped behind her. "I've made arrangements for our entertainment tonight." A sly, eager smile played on her lips. "You know the rules. Dishes. Wear the apron. Nothing else."

Possessive instinct kicked in. I almost said no, but that's what's so appealing about this game we play. So I only nodded. My body throbbed in need, anticipation making it difficult to stifle the urge to ask what she had planned, both for me and him. She takes the lead when we indulge in this fantasy.

I follow.

The doorbell rang moments later, and she ran to answer like she was expecting an important delivery. He barely acknowledged me when he came in before she took his hand and led him down the hall. The bedroom they disappeared into has a direct line of sight into the kitchen. I'm not allowed to look, but I did. Their eyes flayed me raw as I stripped bare and donned the pink gingham apron. The whole dainty thing barely comes to mid-thigh, and when it's tied around my waist in a neat bow, the ends dangle, tickling my ass.

My heart pounds, eagerness tight in my throat. Would this be the day I get recognized? This be the time I finally see a grainy picture of myself trending on social media? Just the *idea* of the degrading questions and interviews; the jeering, snide posts; the whispered ridicule of my peers... Every square inch of my face burns, and I look down at the humiliating bulge growing under the tiny scrap of lace-trimmed fabric.

I stand at the sink, my back to them now. The faucet gushes like my wife will around his cock. A little longer until the dishes are submerged, then I can begin. A bubble rises in the sea of dish water, a little rainbow reflection undulating on the surface. I slowly push a finger into the bubble without breaking the tension. The deluge makes the lemony scent of the dish soap waft up and I inhale, settling into the headspace to perform my act of service, cleaning while she's getting dirty with another man.

"You always know exactly what gets me going," she says to him. "*This* is what you do to me. Feel. I'm so wet." Her husky voice carries across the living room. A siren calling out, begging me to crash and drown.

He chuckles, and the sound mocks me. Feeds my green-eyed monster the shame it craves.

The basin's finally full and I plunge my hands into the hot soapy water. I can't resist. A quick peek over my shoulder. The bedroom door is open, the bed positioned perfectly.

Fuck.

They're side by side, his hand buried between her legs. If only I were covered in slick from her pussy instead of dish water... My hips stutter forward, and I grind my chubbed-up cock against the front of the cabinet. I can't help it. *No*. If I want any relief, I must play by the rules.

Do they steal glances at me as well? Want to see me put in my place? Are they enjoying my indignity? My bare ass faces them as I toil at the sink, on display for her and the one fucking her.

The first dish I find is a cereal bowl, and I wring the sponge out before swiping it over the ceramic. The spray I use to rinse it is just the wrong side of hot, my skin tingling as the heat burns. I can take it.

The bed creaks once, twice, and my breath quickens when I glance back as they lay down. I grab a fork, sliding the sponge over the tines.

"Is this all for me?" he asks.

"Why do you think I texted you? It's not like *he's* satisfying me." She giggles, and tremors tease down my spine all the way to my toes at the disgrace. My cock continues to thicken, and I exhale a shaky breath. Of course she wants someone more masculine, more virile, more—*more*—than me.

Another plate, then a coffee mug. I concentrate on scrubbing her lipstick from the edge of the ceramic, a detailed imprint of her lower lip in scarlet. Her perfect pout I once believed was all for me. Today her lips are for him, and only mine when she believes I've earned it. Is she wearing lipstick? Will she leave a crimson ring at the base of his dick when she sucks him all the way down? A stain on his white collar? Or will she reapply it so when he kisses her, the evidence of their violation—their passion—smears over both their faces, undeniable when I inevitably peek at them, reveling in the sticky shame of it?

I clench the sponge, my hand nearly cramping as I rein in my envy. Soon.

"Get up here," he orders. The bed frame knocks against the wall and I pivot, bare feet sliding on the cold stone tile. My eyes dart back to the bedroom. I'm desperate to see, and desperate not to get caught. He gets comfortable, fluffing my pillow. "Climb on, sweetheart. I want you to sit on my face."

"Yes," she says, her voice gone all breathy. "Own my pussy." I stand still, slightly turned to watch, eager to catch every little sound. The bed springs give as she knee-walks up to where he's spread out across the middle of our king size, occupying my spot and hers. Possessing both her, and the bed. Then, his face is buried between her silky thighs. He's kissing her *there*, probably tongue-fucking her, lapping her juices, sucking her swollen clit like I know she loves. Maybe he's fingering her, pressing one, two, even three inside, stretching her cunt wide, but I can't see from this angle. I shouldn't be looking anyway.

My breath quickens and I turn back to my task, fishing in the sudsy water. Her moan cuts me deep, a reminder that she'd denied me.

When she's with me, she lies on her back, pillow under her bottom, lithe legs spread so I can feast on her pussy while her strong thighs tremble around my ears. Or we sixty-nine, her body covering me. Her gorgeous ass hovers over my face and I suck her as she leans in to tease my cockhead with her tongue. With him, she's all about the show as much as the sensation, displaying herself like she's gagging for it. I shiver, knowing he's the one giving her what she's begging for.

"Oh—oh yeah, right there," she cries out. He groans, and the wooden headboard bangs against the wall. "Fuck..." she trails off on a sigh.

A dinner plate finds its way into my hand. The sponge needs more dish soap, and when I take my hand out of the water to grasp the bottle, my fingers are pink and wrinkled. I bite off a moan—the last time I'd pleasured her, she'd been so wet my fingers looked exactly like this afterward. And there was that time her hot mouth and tongue laved the fingers I used to gag her into silence as we fucked in a bathroom at a friend's lavish holiday party, no one the wiser.

I can almost smell the musk of her pussy instead of the citrus soap.

I can't hold back any longer, reaching under the apron to cup myself with a warm damp hand, grinding against my grip. The tip of my cock is wet and it slides against my palm, slick and easy as anything. My fingers don't feel quite as good as when she's wrapped around me, but it's still relief. I'm shamefully close to coming already, like an inexperienced virgin hoping he doesn't blow his load before getting to fuck for the first time.

"How's it going in there?" he calls from the bedroom.

Delicious humiliation shrouds me as I yank my hand back and swallow hard like I'd been caught reaching into the cookie jar. Maybe I have—I don't check to see if he's watching me. "It's, uh, going fine," I say.

"Almost done?" he asks.

"No," I tell him, fishing in the sudsy basin to assess my task. Halfway through.

"You keep doing your chores like a good boy while I fuck your wife, making her come the way she needs to," he says and laughs. "She's gushing already. Can you hear it?" He does something—maybe plunges his fingers in and out of her—and the sloppy, visceral sounds of her juices slink from the bedroom and down the hallway. The musical tones of her giggle chime in before morphing to a guttural groan, and my bare skin warms under the apron.

I pull a spatula from the sink. It's entirely silicone and has a thick handle. We've played a bit with impact toys before. Her ass would look so tempting, reddened by swat after swat. Or maybe I can fuck her with the handle—it's slimmer than my cock, thinner than anything she'd be used to taking. But maybe that would be the novelty of it.

The bedroom goes strangely quiet. I'm tempted to peek, but if I get caught looking, especially by her, I might lose my chance to clean her up. I wash several spoons, then a tea saucer. Part of her favorite set. I swirl the sponge around the decorative gold edge, like I'll do to her nipples with my tongue tonight. If she lets me. If she hasn't had her fill with him first.

Is he worshipping her tits like I do? Kissing from her collarbone down the center of her chest, teasing the curve of each breast before deciding whether to taunt the left or right first? My cock drips, staining the apron, as I imagine taking a tight peak between my lips, nipping the hard flesh before sucking a mark on the side of her tit with my mouth. There'd be no "gentle" from me tonight.

The saucer's matching teacup rises from the depths. I have to be extra careful that something so precious and fragile doesn't get accidentally damaged. Unlike the scarlet-tinged coffee cup, this one only has a trace of light pink on the lip. Soft. Delicate. Deceptively so. I smile. She's all of those things and none of them.

I cleanse the teacup of every trace of her lip gloss, holding the bone china under the flowing faucet before gently setting it on the drain board. As I pull another dinner plate from the soapy water, I finally hear what I've been waiting for—the staccato slap of skin against skin. My stomach burns, and I stifle a growl that nearly becomes a moan.

The bed gets in on the action, frame ramming the wall, mattress squeaking... I barely have a moment to picture them together, how they're positioned, before she's saying, "Sit up, lean against—yeah."

I need to see.

I turn as the deep blue duvet crumples to the floor with a *thwump*. He's leaning against the headboard while she hovers over his lap facing him, sliding up and down on his cock like she needs it to live, grunting with each thrust, throwing her head back when her body stretches around his girth.

The rhythmic rocking of the furniture and their fucking fills my ears, fueling a rush of sexual jealousy. My heart pounds against my ribcage, the sound mixing with the percussion already being played. I force myself back to work. Maybe he's helping her reach her pleasure, grabbing her ass and tugging her forward, grinding her fat clit against him. Or sliding his fingers between her cheeks, lower, lower, down, down, until he reaches her other entrance, that furled pink hole he'll tease with brushes of fingertips until she cries and begs, tears streaming down her face.

I can't tell what dish I choose next, or the one after. Only that soon the sink is empty and the drain board is full. As though in a trance, I dry my hands and cross the living room to the threshold of the bedroom.

They've shifted and now she's facing me, her back to him as she rides his cock on the rumpled sheets in the center of the bed, kneeling but leaning back, her hands on his abs to support herself. The room is filled with the musky scent of sweat, perfume, and pussy. His hands caress her breasts from behind, playing with her nipples. His hips hitch up, filling her with each thrust, and each time he pulls out the sight of his dick coated in her wetness drives me closer to the edge.

I enter the room and stand there, hands clasped behind

my back. Waiting like a good boy until they're done. Until *he's* done with her.

I want my turn.

Need it.

Will she let me? Will she want me?

"Just like that," she breathes, pushing her sweaty hair off her face with one hand.

He keeps his pace but firms his movements, jarring her body with each deep pump. She throws herself forward, hands on his shins, and *grinds*. Screams. Shakes. Satisfied.

I never tire of watching her in the throes of pleasure. I gorge on this indulgence like a seven-course meal.

He waits until her trembling stops, then whispers, "Turn around, sweetheart. I'm gonna use you."

She slips off his erection, pivots, and hovers over him on her hands and knees. He takes himself in hand and pushes just the head inside. His cock glistens where they're connected, tucked part way into her. His heavy balls are pulled high, granite-hard and ready to pump her full of cum. He lifts his head from the pillow, meeting my gaze, and fucking grins. Arousal and rage race through my veins, and my teeth actually ache with the shame of it. Then he folds his legs up, feet flat on the bed, gaining leverage—and pistons into her braced body. My own dick throbs, like I can feel her clenching me instead of him. He circles an arm around her waist, offering support, as his hips jack up and he empties into her with a long groan.

They both go slack, marionettes with their strings cut, and kiss for a minute like they've forgotten I'm there. My mouth twists and I stand stiffly, focusing on the crumpled duvet on the floor as the embarrassment of being ignored, cast aside, blooms heavy in my gut.

Finally, she rolls off him. "Well?" she asks. I raise my chin. They're both staring at me, heavy, expectant.

"Dishes are done," I tell them.

"Oh my god, the *apron*," she says to him, a mocking smile playing on her lips as she points at me. "He's *so hard*."

My body flames as I turn my gaze down. The apron's tented forward by my swollen erection, and I bite my lip as I move a hand to the front and push it down to no avail. I shift awkwardly, but the tiny panel of pink fabric does nothing to hide the steely flesh.

"Aw, he's shy," he says, while stroking her arm. As he sweeps his fingers down, he teases a nipple back to a hard peak. She grunts and grinds against his hip. He licks his thumb and circles her areola until she rolls away slightly, letting him access her other breast.

He meets my eyes again and my skin breaks out into goosebumps. "I fuckin' wore her out, but maybe she'll give you a ride. Since you finished the dishes and all. What do you think, sweetheart?" He pinches her nipple. "Might help tide you over 'til I pump this pussy full again."

She appraises me, an eyebrow raised. "Yeah, I guess so."

"Well, don't just stand there," he says to me.

I nod bashfully and I take my apron off. A silky string of precum connects my dick to the apron. The crown is so wet, I'm surprised it doesn't drip on the floor. "Clean it off," she instructs.

My face is hot with shame as I bring the apron to my mouth and lick the sodden fabric. Only when there's no trace of my arousal left do I fold it, setting it on a chair. The air is cool on my naked body. My cock bobs when I move, and I stroke myself once. The momentary pleasure almost—almost—hurts, and I clamp my eyes closed, getting ahold of myself. They'd love to see me come early, spilling into my fist or on her ass or pussy lips before I can even get inside her, but I have to maintain some dignity. They'd never let me inside her again if I humiliate myself like that—I'm a good boy who does what she wants.

She climbs over him toward me, dragging her chest across his as she turns around to face the center of the bed, knees digging into the edge of the mattress. As I step closer, she stares at me over her shoulder and spreads her legs wider, arching her back to give me a good view. Her cunt is flushed and swollen, clit plump and eager as it peeks from its hood. A trickle of semen runs from her hole.

I grasp my dripping cock and shuffle toward her.

"Nuh uh." She shakes her head, an eyebrow raised at me. "First, clean me." Her ass and pussy pulse as she bears down, pushing another gush of cum out. It slips toward her clit and I catch it in my mouth as the stream surrounds the fat nub. I lick it, tasting them together, salt and musk. I want to rub it all over myself, wear them like cologne.

I slurp at her cunt, working the tip of my tongue through her folds, getting every stray drop. I flick my tongue rapidly over the meat of her, jiggling her sensitive flesh, grinning against her when she backs into my face, thirsting for more. Then I trail up to the source— where she's dripping with it.

Fuck, there's so much. How many times did he fill her? Doesn't matter. I'm here now, and she's gonna get filled again. I jab my tongue into her as deep as I can get. She's so hot and wet, and I can't even tell what's her or him anymore. I groan and hold her hips with wide, shaking hands as I scoop it out of her with my mouth. Every second or third time, after I've swallowed, I pause to give her clit a little suck. She leans back onto my face again, but this time I pull away.

My cue is the little nod she gives me over her shoulder. I push between her shoulder blades and she lowers her upper body obediently. Did he take her from behind like this tonight? Has he before? Will he next time?

I line up and bury myself in her, ready to erase any evidence he'd had her already.

She's still tight even though she already took cock tonight. Each thrust shoves me closer to filling her with a well-earned load, and I need to take her with me, need to earn my spot in her roster. I reach around and tweak her clit between two fingers, jerking the hood around the hard nub. She wails and grinds into my hand and I give her what she craves.

She screams my name, voice cracking, as her muscles milk my dick.

I possessively wrap my fingers in her hair and pull back, making her arch even more. My hips stutter and I roar, resentment and envy pouring out when my balls tighten and I finally reclaim what's mine, cock jerking inside her with each stream of cum.

He moves to one side of the bed as she and I collapse on the mattress and I pull her close, tucking her head under my chin and kissing her hair. He chastely kisses each of us, a reminder of a job well done as he pulls back. We all catch our breath, then he climbs off the mattress and gets dressed.

"See you same time next month?" he asks, standing in the doorway with his coat thrown over an arm. He waits hesitantly until I lean up on an elbow and nod.

"Absolutely," I say.

She hums, squeezing my wrist and stroking the soft skin there. He grins and heads out.

We doze for a bit, sated for the time being. Soon she yawns and kisses my neck. "Can we order in tonight?" she says, a smile playing on her lips. "You pick. Wouldn't want to dirty too many dishes."

Teacher Pet

Grading papers is stressful for every teacher, but when she loses focus, Pet's Mistress will give her what she needs—instructions, rules, and discipline. The only thing that matters is obeying Mistress.

Pairing: FF

Tropes: married couple / established couple, sapphic spice, married lesbians, toys in the bedroom, BDSM, consensual power dynamics, soft femdom / gentle femdom, make me stop thinking so much, pet names

Teacher Pet

I scrawled a C- in red ink on the first page of the essay and tossed it on top of the growing pile of papers. Twelve more to go. I swiped my hands over my face, careful to not smear my eye makeup. My high school Brit Lit students were trying to do me in. I loved waxing poetic about Shakespeare, Austen, and Dickens, and tried my best to instill an appreciation in them in modern teenagers. Still, I held down a scream of frustration at the ridiculousness of their interpretations of great literature. At least the papers on Chaucer were entertaining—watching the students dance around his racier content was almost worth having to slog through the grading.

I sipped my coffee and made a face as the tepid liquid slid down my throat.

At least a bottle of my favorite whisky awaited as soon as my pen scribbled the grade on the last one.

But for now I'd have to settle for my snack if I had any hope of finishing. The ruby red apple was smooth in my fingers as I turned it to find the best place to sink my teeth. I opened my mouth. Bit down. The flavor burst on my tongue, sharp and tangy. I gazed at the apple, juices pouring from the perfect bite mark, and I licked the cool skin, catching every drop.

Just like when Mistress puts me on my knees, her hand gripping my hair, my tongue buried in her—

I squeezed my legs together as heat built in my core.

If only we had time to play today...

No. I shoved the thought away. I had work to do.

Time to get on with it. I grabbed the next essay—another one on Tolkien—and prepared to deploy my red pen of doom. But the words swam on the page as my focus drained.

"Hey." My gaze lifted to the door of the home office where Raquel stood. Her wedding ring caught the sunlight, and my face split into a grin. I'd never get tired of seeing it.

"Ready for a break?" she asked. "You've been at it for hours." She hooked her thumbs in the pockets of her jeans and leaned against the doorframe. The weight of her hands pulled the denim down her slim waist, sliding over her hip bones, lower, lower...

I sighed and sank down in my office chair. "I wish this were a poison apple. Then I wouldn't have to finish."

Raquel eyed the ungraded stack and cocked a perfect eyebrow. "Break it is, mi amor, if you're already wishing for death. Especially Snow-White-style."

I winced. "This is my job. They're due back Monday. I can't—"

"Can't?" Raquel shifted, straightening her spine and crossing her arms. "Get up."

My eyes widened at her command. "But—"

"Don't speak, and don't make me repeat myself." Her dark eyes were intense. "Nod if you understand and want to continue, Pet."

I melted, every inch of my skin and soul warm, betraying the hold she had over me and how much I craved it. *Hell yeah.* I shivered, my arms breaking out in goosebumps. The chair slid away from the desk as I stood.

Raquel turned and strode out into the hall. I followed, the familiar sense of sweeping calm and perfect resignation flowing over me as Raquel—now Mistress—dominated every conscious thought.

She stopped a few steps away from our bedroom door. "Are you wearing the gray camisole and panty set I laid out for you this morning?"

"Yes, Mistress." I loved dressing up for her. The soft material, edged in lace, made me feel so feminine.

"Good. Strip down to that." She grabbed my hand and dragged me forward, taking my lips in a fierce kiss, making me forget anything that wasn't her.

She backed away, her eyes already peeling my clothes off. "I want you kneeling on the floor when I come in. And put on the blindfold." She directed me into the bedroom with a firm shove.

I scrambled to obey, holding my breath at the rush of handing control over to the one I loved. The bedroom door clicked closed behind me. I tore my pants and shirt off, folded them neatly, then retrieved the blindfold from our toy box. My heart raced as I sank into position, kneeling and slipping the dark fabric over my eyes. The world disappeared, tugging my stress away with it. I clasped my hands behind my back. I would hold the pose as long as required. Mistress would take her time. Make me wait. Make me forget why I was stressed. Make me regain focus, thinking about nothing but her.

I inhaled, and everything narrowed down to what I could hear, touch, taste, smell—something Mistress exploited to both of our enjoyment. I fucking loved it.

Just when my knees started to ache, soft footsteps drew closer, and the door opened. "Good girl." Mistress's voice was full of gentle pride and I flushed with the praise. "Just how I wanted you."

A finger tipped my chin up, and her full lips pressed against mine. She kissed me like we had all the time in the world. Like she would make time stop, just for me. She stroked my jaw, my neck, my collarbone with her fingertips. The cami pulled taut over my chest as she grabbed the straps behind my back and my fingers grappled with each other, struggling to stay where they should be. I barely reined in the groan in my throat when she released me.

More. I needed more.

"Greedy girl," she said, patting my cheek. "I'll take care of you, Pet. I always do."

The heat of her body moved away, and I clung to the residual fire. The quiet whisper of clothing being removed, the muffled thumps as the items hit the floor, deepened the heavy ache between my legs. My pebbled nipples strained for the touch they'd missed out on.

"What shall we use today, Pet?" The toy box opened as she spoke, the squeak of the hinges full of promises. "The silk scarves? Handcuffs? Perhaps the wooden paddle... Oh, I know—perfect."

I shifted my weight, leaning toward the rustling until the noise paused. I wiggled back in place, but not quickly enough. Strong fingers wound through my hair, pulling up until it stung, lifting my face. My jaw went slack.

"Stay. Still," Raquel said, right in front of me, warm breath on my skin. Her scent was sweet, like raspberries and her morning coffee. "Nod if you understand."

I strained against her painful grip just enough to move my head.

Her hand disappeared, my scalp tingling at the release of pressure.

Out of nowhere, something firm and flexible touched one of my nipples, tapping the hard nub over the cami. I jolted, then relaxed into it. The scent of leather wafted upward as she moved the small riding crop— my favorite toy, the touch of the cowhide as familiar as

Mistress's fingers, but never as satisfying—circling each breast, then trailing it over my neck and face. Oh yes...

From the first time we hooked up, she'd been obsessed with my tits. Touching them, rubbing them, feeling the weight of them in her hands. Thumbing over my pink-brown nipples, desperate to make them stand out, plump and hard, before she'd run her lips over them and taunt me with teeth and tongue until I was a sobbing mess.

But the sensation of the cool leather was far different from being touched or pinched with a finger—impersonal, like I was something to be used. I craved it. Because, when we played, I existed only for Mistress's pleasure. And her pleasure was wringing every drop of mine out of me.

My pussy gushed as the crop—an extension of Mistress, as if it were her own fingers trailing my skin —brushed my collarbone. Back and forth. Up my throat. Over my open mouth. I shivered, going breathless as I anticipated the leather's sting.

My jaw relaxed just a little bit more and the crop traced my lips, light as a feather.

"Careful," Mistress warned, though her tone was teasing. "Or I'll give you something to fill it. And I'll be so disappointed if I can't hear you because you're gagged."

Down my neck again, then a figure eight around my breasts. Closer and closer to where I needed her...

A moan slipped out, and I bit my lips to suppress the urge to beg.

Fingers grabbed my jaw, tilting my head back. "You have permission to come when you need to, as many times as you need to. And I want to *hear* you. You make the most beautiful sounds, Pet."

A whine, desperate and needy, flowed from my throat, and the cami was shoved up over each tit. Mistress rolled a nipple between her fingers in reward, her murmured words full of praise.

Over and over the tip of the crop teased, the supple leather so much more flexible than the acrylic paddle, more rigid than our feather tickler, moving from one exposed nipple to the other. Tapping, sliding, nudging. Never enough, yet almost too much. I could feel how tight they were, how eager and hard. Almost painful. Fuck, I wanted her mouth, her lips... I tried to imagine what the furled buds would look like, reddened and plump, ready for her to suck...

"Look at your tits," she breathed, but she left the blindfold where it was. "Remember when I took you out last summer? You were so obedient—no bra, the thin shirt, just like I asked."

My mind wandered to that date night. But my memories weren't of the sweltering heat or the meal we ate, but of the way she'd teased and played with me in the car where *anyone* could have seen, stroking my body like an instrument.

Mistress brought me back to myself, the caresses evolving into sharper slaps that left behind a light sting. My clit throbbed, so much closer to the edge than I expected to be. If she kept it up, I'd come just from this. And she knew it.

Pleasure threatened to overtake me, and I breathed into every touch and sensation. I had to hold off. Make it last.

One breath. *Slap.* Two. *Slap.* Three. *Slap.* Oh *fuck*...

Gravity seemed to give way and I left my body behind, hanging in suspended animation.

Then a single finger on each nipple. Circling, circling, so, so gentle, almost an apology, but one she certainly didn't mean, and one I absolutely didn't want. One hand deserted a breast, only to reappear a second later at my thighs, urging them apart. Slowly I separated my knees, and then a finger caressed my clit through my underwear. I whimpered.

"Oh, you're close, aren't you, Pet. Stay just like that. I want to feel your clit pulse when it happens."

She pulled the cami back down, my breasts so sensitive I could feel every thread of fabric. Warm wetness surrounded a covered nipple, soaking the thin material as she suckled, worrying the hard tip with her lips and trapping the other peak between two fingers. The hand between my legs was just a whisper of a touch. Tension gathered in my thighs as I resisted the urge to grind down on her fingers, held myself perfectly still so Mistress wouldn't stop. In a flash she switched breasts, wetting the other side while she flicked the damp nub with a fingernail.

A flicker of shame hit then, from somewhere deep down—how dirty this was, how I should be a good girl, how I shouldn't want to feel this—but I was *Mistress's* good girl. I inhaled a shuddering breath, drawing comfort from her scent. Everything I was belonged to her. If she wanted me to feel it, I would. Because she knew what I loved. What made me feel good. And there was nothing wrong with that.

"Ohhh," I moaned, breath catching on the long exhale. My clit ached as her tongue urged the tight nipple to stiffen even more. The pad of one finger tormented the other, and when she expertly rolled it between two fingers, it was all over.

I cried out, hot, quaking. A single finger slipped around the side of my panties and inside my pussy, coaxing the last tremors of my orgasm out of me. Feeling the wetness, the quivering, the fruits of her labors. What she did to me. How only she gave me what I needed. How bound to her I was.

I was Pet.

Owned by Mistress.

Rushing blood and ragged breaths filled my ears and the scent of my arousal surrounded me.

"That's it, Pet. Let me take care of you." The finger filling me crooked a little, and she probed around my opening some more. Perfunctory, impersonal. Using me. I squirmed, the wet skin bordering on oversensitivity. "No, you're done when *I* decide you're done," Mistress said. Teeth captured one of my nipples, pinching the bud. I groaned and my breath hitched, then a soothing tongue calmed the sting.

"Oh, you're perfect," she said. "Tight little nipples, swollen wet pussy. And your clit—it gets so hard for me."

I sobbed and she hummed. I could practically hear her satisfied smile. My spine straightened and I proudly thrust my chest out, happy to have pleased her.

"Up." The hand between my legs pushed, like it was lifting me. I wobbled as I rose to my feet, the lack of vision throwing me only slightly off balance. Her fingers crawled up my belly, then curled around the elastic of my underwear. She tugged, her short nails scratching as she inched the cotton over my hips and down my thighs. A puff of air hit my wet slit when I raised each foot in turn to step out of them. "Turn to your right, hands on the bed, and spread your legs. I want to see what I do to you."

My face flushed. The slower I moved, the more I could feel her eyes on me, like there was a spotlight following my every shuffling step toward the bed. The tips of my fingers touched first, rippling the cool, silky duvet as I stretched my arms out.

"Wider." She shoved my legs apart and applied a grounding pressure on my upper back so my chest was on the bed. "Stay," she ordered, petting a warm hand all the way down to my ass. I rubbed my burning cheek against the sleek fabric, enjoying the feeling of being taken care of. Of leaving society's conventions behind. Of having someone else make the decisions.

The bed shifted and a finger nudged my mouth. "Suck."

I obediently opened for the finger—the same one that had been in my body. I lapped at it, licking my essence from her skin.

"Good, Pet, that's enough," she said, stroking my long hair, massaging my scalp with her fingertips. "You deserve a reward for being so obedient."

The slap of her hand across my ass made me squeal and I tensed all over, barely catching myself before I moved away. Smacks rained down on both cheeks, heating my skin as the blood rushed to the surface. Mistress got into a rhythm, the sting lingering longer, coming quicker. I couldn't catch my breath, and I flipped like a switch to float away, leaving my body behind for Mistress to tend to.

"Give me your color," she said, her voice low and husky.

A stoplight flashed through my mind, only one light glowing brightly. "Green, oh my god, I'm so green," I slurred against the duvet. Her hand stroked my back for a moment.

Leather swatted along my hot flesh. No inch of my backside was spared. The swoosh of the crop swinging through the air, the lingering bite of each impact, and gentle, whispered appreciation from Mistress...it all cocooned me in that wonderful floaty feeling.

The crop slowed, giving way again to hands kneading my reddened cheeks. She had to be able to feel how hot the skin was. I groaned, long and relieved.

"Gorgeous," she whispered, and the mattress dipped as she leaned on the bed next to me. "Your ass is scarlet, just like that apple you were eating." Her hand slid to my pussy again, two fingers slipping inside, anchoring me for just a moment, snug and safe in her touch. "So wet. Dripping. My little tart. My little apple tart."

My whole being hummed at the words, reaching a resonant frequency that only Raquel—even as Mistress—could tune into.

She rubbed up my side, pushed off the mattress, and dropped to the floor. She split my cheeks. Cool air found my swollen flesh. "How pretty, all this juicy pink."

My face heated but then her tongue was on me, then in me, feasting. Dipping inside. The two fingers returned, opening me up while she explored my body, thrusting and separating. Pleasure coiled like a spring, a tight knot low in my abdomen. Smooth lips sealed over my clit and gently sucked until I released, clenching her fingers and screaming into the bed until, eventually, my heaving breath slowed.

"Blindfold off." The snick of the lube cap echoed. "On the bed, face up." A buckle clinked as it was locked into place. "Spread wide so I can see that sweet little hole before I fuck it full." Leather creaked with tension.

Oh god, she knew exactly what to say to turn me even more desperate. My shaky legs barely held my weight as I stood, flopped onto the mattress, and ripped the blindfold off. The room was unnaturally bright and I blinked, eyes adjusting. I propped myself up on my elbows, and my mouth popped open.

Mistress was completely nude, miles of sensuous tan skin on display as she slid one end of a violet double-ended dildo inside her pussy, pulsing it a couple of times before she finished buckling the leather harness around it. Oh *fuck me*. This toy. It was so fucking big, but I loved it. The stretch. The length. The well-placed veins. I was about to get a *ride*.

She slicked up the purple shaft. Then she shook the bottle at me. More? *Yes, please.* I'd need all the help I could get to handle that silicone cock and the woman wielding it. "Please, Mistress," I said, voice already wrecked. Her rosy lips curled up in a sexy smirk.

"Good girl." She came over and hooked her hands under my knees, scooting me right to the edge of the bed. My legs fell open the rest of the way.

A drizzle of cool lube hit my slit, and she worked it into my pussy with two fingers. She teased my opening with her fingertips until I was so close to begging, eager to be filled up. But begging was talking, and there was no way I would do anything to stop Mistress before I took every inch of that cock.

Mistress brought a hand down to guide the dildo, pressing the head into my pussy. My muscles stretched around the flared tip, burning with the delicate dance of pain and pleasure as she moved, working more of the shaft inside.

Running hands up my trembling thighs, scratching red lines down my abdomen, roughly rubbing my arms, she touched me everywhere. Soon she'd pushed all the way in, but the silicone cock pressed in too far. I tensed, back arched.

Mistress paused immediately. "Color?"

"Yellow. Too deep." The dildo withdrew a fraction and the pressure lessened, leaving my cunt hungry. I clenched around her cock, walls rippling, dying to fuck it. One of her hands was wrapped around the base of the toy, giving her more control of the depth.

"How about now?"

"Green, Mistress." And so, so safe. Treasured. Taken care of.

She lowered her head and kissed me, her warm tongue and that cock of hers plunging in with the same rhythm. She fucked me *oh* so good, pumping and filling me almost too much, the dildo parting my body like she was born to do it. We were covered in lube and my juices, and the obscene sounds accompanying her quick thrusts filled the room.

Mistress cupped the back of my head, weaving her long fingers through my hair, her tight grip holding me exactly where she wanted. My legs widened, urging her to take everything I had to give. Greedy for everything she'd give me. Low, eager moans vibrated between us.

She ruled my mouth as she paused to grind the base of her cock on my cunt, groaning as she hit both her sweet spots and mine. I gasped when she swiveled her hips. Right there. Oh my god. The pressure grew, almost too much, and my eyes rolled back. Mistress grinned into our kiss and found the familiar pattern that did me in.

"Oh! Oh oh *oh*..." The orgasm crested and flowed, sweeping me down a river of pleasure. Her hips stilled, pressing against me, and Mistress grasped my hair tighter as she followed me over the edge, her own head thrown back in ecstasy. One of my hands trailed down to where the harness and dildo met to touch Mistress's wet pussy, to feel the pleasure she'd gotten from pleasing me—but I stopped myself. Our play time today wasn't about that.

Still coming down from my high, I barely registered Raquel pulling out and unfastening the harness before throwing herself on the bed next to me. I stared at the ceiling, hardly able to move a muscle.

She flung an arm over my exhausted body, holding me close. "Better, mi amor?"

"I barely remember who I am right now," I murmured, focusing on her beaming face. "What was I doing before this?"

She laughed, full and throaty. "My job here is done."

"Oh, wait." I snapped my fingers. "Grading. I was grading those awful interpretation essays. Why do I assign those stupid things every year? Am I just a glutton for punishment?"

"Yes. Yes you are." Raquel grinned, her eyes full of mirth.

I groaned, covering my face with my arms.

"Uh oh." Raquel propped herself up on an elbow, gazing down at me. "Looks like you're stressed again."

"Maybe. Can't really tell. But we can't take any chances, right?" I asked, drawing her down for another kiss.

Third Time's the Charm

Jamie's reflection in the yoga studio's mirror finally matches who she is. And when her cute blond dream woman flirts back during yoga class, Jamie's ready to explore how flexible she can be.

Pairing: FF

Tropes: sapphic spice, trans woman and cis woman, yoga instructor, trainer / student, first time in a long time, shower fun, wet and wild, body acceptance, semi-public sex

Third Time's the Charm

The first time it happened was between my legs in downward dog.

I was in my usual spot—last row, right-hand corner in front of the yoga studio's walls of mirrors—when my eyes met those of the woman next to me in the tight pink capris. Between *her* legs. In the mirror. She didn't look away, even quirking an eyebrow at me while the instructor guided us into three-legged dog. A flush heated my body, and I glanced down at my mat. She's gorgeous. No way did she look at me like *that*. Would it happen again?

The second time, it was in cobra. The instructor had us hold the pose, shaking our heads gently left and right. Our eyes locked, neither of us moving. Hers were a stunning sapphire, somehow fitting with her tied-up, long blond hair.

She wore a light blue top with a built-in bra—I couldn't see lines. What I could see, though, were tight, eager nipples pushing shamelessly against the fabric. I turned in the other direction and caught the image of my own achy breasts in the mirror, my new reflection unfamiliarly perfect.

I rotated back and Hot Yoga Neighbor's eyes skipped down to my chest. Straight white teeth sank into her juicy bottom lip, and I wanted nothing more than for it to be *my* teeth instead. Butterflies invaded my stomach, fluttering in a way I hadn't experienced since college. Oh yeah, this was a full-on crush. Was the feeling mutual? The instructor changed poses, and I wanted to yell in frustration.

The third time—standing wide-legged forward fold. Bent at the waist, legs spread with my hands flat on the floor, head hanging. Her gaze greeted mine in the mirror, upside down between her toned, pink-clad thighs. *Please* let my ass look as good as hers.

Her lips mouthed: "Wait for me."

My breath caught, tight in my chest—was I reading her right? Still upside down, I nodded, my stomach clenched with anticipation. We straightened, standing tall and upright in mountain pose, and I had to shake my long, chestnut ponytail from my face, exhaling to puff away some stray hair. I snuck a glance to my left, pleased when the corners of her mouth quirked up. Lovely.

I barely noticed the rest of the poses for the remainder of the session, following along like a robot while fantasizing. But at the end of class, just as I turned toward her, Hot Yoga Neighbor walked away to talk to the instructor.

Wait. What if...

I took a few deep, centering breaths. I couldn't control what happened. If she changed her mind, there was nothing I could do.

I rolled my mat and drank from my water bottle, adjusted my flowy tank top, packed and repacked my bag just to have something for my hands to do, to keep them from trembling.

As I watched, Hot Yoga Neighbor nodded to the instructor and returned to her mat. I towered over her by several inches, even barefoot. She tilted her chin up, tongue briefly peeking from between her lips as she appraised me. Flustered, I adjusted my tote so it hooked more comfortably over one shoulder.

"Hi," she said, her smile growing to a grin as she extended a hand. "I'm Megan. Nice pin." She tapped the little light blue, pink, and white trans flag attached to my tote bag.

"Jamie. And thanks." I took her hand. Her skin was soft, her fingers long, elegant; each manicured nail painted a pretty baby pink. "I've seen you here before. You're...busy."

"You could say that. I'm one of the co-owners of the studio." Megan did that lip-biting thing that had turned me inside out before. "I observe the classes and do one-on-ones. In fact"—she shifted her hand out from mine, settling it on my bicep—"I usually have one now. But my student cancelled."

"That's too bad."

Megan tipped her head to the side, the corner of her lips teasing a playful smile for a moment as the last of the class left the room. "Not really." The hand on my bicep—holy shit, she hadn't let go—squeezed.

"So...you have...free time?" Was my voice shaky?

Her blue eyes bored into my dark brown ones. "Would you like to see where we do private sessions?"

My skin ignited and warm, wet heat pooled low in my belly. I nodded.

Megan's sapphire eyes slowly traveled from my face down my chest to where my loose top ended at my upper thighs and my clit pressed against my yoga pants, twitching as she stared.

Time stopped.

My mouth went dry as a desert, but I summoned courage and said quietly, "I haven't had bottom surgery."

The words hung in the air in the otherwise empty room. I met her eyes, her heated gaze unchanged.

"Not an issue." Then Megan took my hand. "Come with me? You can leave those here."

I nodded and dropped my tote and mat. We walked down a short hall hand in hand while I tried desperately not to overthink this. I hadn't exactly been—involved? Intimate?—with many people since beginning my transition.

Before I could say anything, Megan led me through a wooden door with a translucent, frosted glass inset that glowed in the soft lighting. The room smelled faintly of sandalwood; the floor covered with black gym mats.

We stopped in the middle of the room.

Close. So close.

The blue of her eyes was nearly swallowed by black pupils, and her breath came in little pants between parted lips. One of her hands returned to my upper arm and the other mirrored it, thumbs caressing my skin. I broke out in goosebumps.

"Is this okay?" she whispered.

"Yes."

The kiss was a frantic crash of lips, as much tongue and teeth as it was tender. I wove a hand around her ponytail, drawing her up on her tiptoes, while she grabbed the loose hair at the nape of my neck, gasping into my mouth.

We sank to the floor. Kneeling, pressed tightly front to front, there was nowhere to hide.

Slowly, confidently, her hand slipped between us, sliding along the full length of me, thumbing the tip. Coiled tension broke when she didn't back away.

"You're so wet," she said against my lips. "How do you want..."

I moved, sitting upright, drawing her in to straddle my lap. Then I leaned back a little, bracing myself on my extended arms. She pushed herself flush against me, her yoga pants warm and damp where she pressed her body to mine. Megan trembled as she used my ponytail to tilt my head. I cried into her mouth as she executed a filthy, full-body roll.

The musky scent of our arousal and frantic grunts as we rutted together filled the room. I ground up, pumping my hips, our bodies sliding with the slippery material between us. My fingers clawed the mat, desperately trying to hold onto my last shred of control.

Megan jerked my top down to reveal one of my tits, then pinched the aching nipple. The sharp, sudden sensation shot down my spine and I tugged her lower lip between my teeth as I came, shaking and wetting the slick fabric. She threw her head back, mouth slack, groaning as she rode me, her hips stuttering against the ridge of my clit.

We caught our breath, gently kissing. My hands found their way to her waist, nudging under her shirt to find the silky skin there. Megan stroked her hand down my front, tracing the darkening wet spot on my navy blue leggings. I shivered.

"I've been wanting to have a private lesson with you for a while," she said, laughing. "Your ass in these..."

"Nope—mine's not even close to how good yours looks." I took a deep breath, preparing to shoot my shot. "Would you like to go for coffee?"

She playfully cocked an eyebrow. "Shower first."

"Are there private showers?"

Megan nodded.

"Then lead the way."

After a quick detour to grab my tote and mat from the classroom, Megan guided me down the hallway to a part of the studio I'd never been in. I'd used the locker rooms there a few times, but never the shower facilities.

And, when she opened the door, it was apparent I wouldn't be using the studio's main showers today either.

"Is this your office?" I asked, looking around. The room was Zen in the best way—not overly woo but organized and minimalist. Sage green, lavender, and cream made the space comfortable and calming.

"Yes. I share it with Annabelle, the other owner. But she's not here today." Megan grinned as she brought a hand up to the door lock, then paused. "Is this okay?" she said, glancing at the deadbolt. "This way we won't be interrupted."

My mouth went dry. "God, yes."

The lock slid solidly home. This was happening.

She turned and skirted one of the two desks and entered a doorway on the opposite wall. I followed, heart in my throat. In a few moments, she would be the first person to see me naked in a fun way in a long time. Surprisingly, I was more eager than nervous, though anxiety fluttered in my stomach.

The private bathroom was expansive, fully tiled from floor to ceiling with an enormous, spa-like shower. Spacious. Room to move, to bend, even with two of us in there.

Megan opened the glass shower door and turned the water on. The rainfall showerhead sprayed with enviable water pressure that would feel amazing pounding over my tired muscles.

She stepped away, closing the door behind her. We stood, just staring at each other for a minute, and before awkward could make it all the way to *really* awkward, Megan said, "Okay, I feel like I should come clean here. I don't usually do this"—she gestured between us, and I cocked my head—"I mean..." She closed her eyes and chuckled nervously. "Jeez, I'm bad at this."

"Better than me." I shrugged with one shoulder, only sort of trying to hide what a big deal this was. "It's... been a while."

"Well then, let's be awkward together." Megan took a couple steps toward me. "How about this—every piece of clothing I take off, you have to take off the same one."

I nodded, my face heating.

"And since I proposed this game, I'll start." She reached up and took out her hair elastic, shaking out her long, blond hair as it released from her ponytail.

I snort-laughed, and some of the tension melted away. "That one was a gimmie."

"Gotta start with something." Mock-stern, Megan put her hands on her hips.

I reached up and removed my ponytail tie, chestnut hair falling free.

"See? Not so bad." Her voice was low and husky. She stepped closer again, like someone trying not to spook a shy animal, and carefully tucked a strand of hair behind my ear. The air between us charged and crackled, like dry humping until I came in my pants ten minutes ago didn't even take the edge off.

Slowly, she drew her hands down her torso, grabbing her light blue top at the hem before whipping it over her head. I'd been right—she hadn't been wearing a bra, and her tits were spectacular. Small mounds that were a perfect handful. Plump, pink-brown nipples begged for my mouth.

"Now you," she said, swaying a little side to side on her feet.

I slid my flowy, gray shirt off without delay, tossing it to the side. Then, I waited.

"Nope," she teased, shaking her head and stepping into my space to loop a finger under my bra strap. "That was a two-for-one from me. Lose this, too."

Okay, fair. I wiggled out of my sports bra. Her eyes flicked down to my chest, and she closed the gap between us as though magnets drew us together. Soft lips sealed around one of my nipples as she kissed it, giving the hard flesh a quick suck before pulling away. She rubbed it with her thumb and my clit swelled. "We got acquainted a little earlier," she murmured, my lust-fogged mind flashing to when she'd given that same nipple a pinch, the pleasure-pain shocking with how quickly it made me come. "But I wanted to introduce myself properly."

I needed to feel her under my hands. I took it slow, not wanting to break the rules of this game between us, and set my hands on her hips. My thumbs hooked into her waistband, and when her face held nothing but eagerness, I slid those pink leggings down her hips, her toned legs, then off her feet. The tile was cold under my toes as I stepped back to take her in.

Megan's abs were defined but soft, leading down to a groomed triangle of short, curly, blond hair a little darker than her head. Her legs were long and lean, thighs covered in thin stretch marks I wanted to trace with my tongue while she straddled my face.

Perfect imperfection. Just like me.

"Now you." Her chest heaved, nipples begging like her words.

Despite the warm, steamy room, my arms broke out in goosebumps, anticipation climbing.

"I—would you like to do it for me?" I barely got my tentative words out before she was in my space again, hands bracketing my hips like I'd done to her. Her thumbs circled my hipbones, dip-dip-dipping beneath the folded waistband of my leggings.

Then she paused, biting her lip. This time I didn't hesitate, cupping the back of her head and holding her, brushing a thumb over her lower lip, drawing it out from between her teeth before taking over and sinking mine into the plump flesh. Megan groaned, eyelids fluttering as we kissed, the distraction from my nerves welcome as she worked my navy leggings down and under my ass. My clit snagged on the tight material, and I snuck a hand between us to free myself.

With the two of us busy making out and neither of us looking at what we were doing, it was an Olympic event to get my leggings off. Besides her two hands and the one I didn't have behind her neck, it took far too much time and *way* too much balance, along with just the right amount of laughter. As soon as the fabric hit my feet, I used my heels to step out of them and kicked them toward a wall.

This was it.

As I took a step back, her heavy-lidded eyes followed, sliding from my bare breasts down my stomach to my obvious arousal.

"You're gorgeous." Megan licked her lips. "Can I—would you like me to touch you?"

I nodded eagerly and took her fingers in mine. "Please. Like you'd touch yourself," I told her. I flushed as I guided her to take me in hand, shivering when her fingertips grazed the sensitive flesh. Gently, so, so slowly, she spread my wetness over the tip. I closed my eyes, my mouth dropping open on a sigh. Trails of sparks followed every trace of her hands, lighting me up.

Tentatively her touch wandered behind my clit to stroke the flat patch of skin. Warm arousal built in my belly as I began to really relax, to enjoy. Her fingertips slid up, ringing my clit and giving it a squeeze. My eyes popped open. She winked, then turned to the steamed-up shower and opened the glass door.

"After you," Megan said, gesturing for me to go first. As I passed her on my way in, I grabbed the nape of her neck and claimed her mouth, unable to contain the relief and sheer joy pounding through my veins. When I pulled away she chased me with her lips, following the kiss, and me, into the shower.

Hot water beat down, soaking my long hair. Stiffness melted from my neck and shoulders the longer I stood under the spray. The door closed behind her and the stall clouded with mist again. I inhaled lavender-scented moisture deep into my lungs and sighed it out. Megan turned to face me, droplets of water clinging to her eyelashes, her bottom lip, her breasts. My hands flexed. I had to touch. We crashed together at the same time, running palms over soft skin and taut muscles. Lips sucked and teeth bit.

Still under the spray, I guided Megan to turn around and I pressed myself to her back, plucking and rolling her hard nipples. "Please," she begged, writhing against me.

I licked her neck and bit her jaw. "What do you want?"

"Touch me. Make me come." Her breathy voice and the way she reached back and grabbed one of my ass cheeks broke the last of my restraint. I pinched her tits, pulling the stiff peaks away from her body, only releasing when she gasped and threw her head back, leaning on my shoulder.

I wound my arms around her middle and snaked a hand down her front, trailing my fingertips through her pubic hair before sliding my middle finger between her lower lips, flicking her swollen clit back and forth.

"Yes," she hissed, and arched her back, grinding her backside into my pelvis. Struck with inspiration, I grabbed the conditioner and squirted some on her ass and lower back before resuming our positions, this time with my clit hugged neatly between those juicy cheeks.

"Now, where were we?" I teased in her left ear. I bit the lobe and she backed into me, seamlessly fitting her body to mine. With one hand wrapped around her waist I kept her there as my hand resumed its trek down, down, down. I probed her pussy with my middle and ring finger until I found her channel. Slick and hot, it welcomed me as I worked those two digits into her, the heel of my hand coming to rest on her throbbing clit. She spread her legs even more. An invitation.

Curious and eager, I cupped her cunt, just holding her, marveling. She reached up and held onto the forearm I'd looped around her, long fingers digging in but not trying to dislodge me. Just holding on for the ride.

"Ready?" I asked.

"Fuck, I'm ready for anything," she panted out.

Synchronizing my movements, I ground my hand against her and into her while sliding along the slippery valley of her ass. The channel there was tight and warm as I rubbed on her, not unlike where my fingers fucked her. I trembled against her back.

"Oh my god," she breathed. "Jamie, fuck." She arched into my hand.

"Let me give it to you." Thankful for the strength I'd built during the classes, I pressed her to me, grinding my palm against her. She balanced on one leg, letting the other rest on the low shower bench. Easy access. I sucked her neck and pumped her pussy, tipping closer and closer to the edge with her.

Megan's deep breaths made my grip around her ribs seem even tighter. "So close," she cried out. Her nails bit into my forearm, but the pain only added to the pleasure.

"Me too." I moaned and humped her ass, my sensitive head throbbing, ready to spill.

"Oh—right there." She adjusted her stance slightly. "Right there right there...fuck!" Her cunt gripped me, a rhythmic vice. Her clit pulsed, twitching against my palm. I crushed her to me, determined to keep her upright through the throes.

Just knowing I'd made her come was enough to finish me off. I drove into that tight valley a few more times before I sprayed cum onto her soft skin. A feral part of me loved that I'd marked her, and when I'd finished easing her through her orgasm, I gently pulled my fingers from her and sucked her essence from them to mark myself.

We collapsed to the shower floor, warm water running around us. I held her until she stopped quivering.

Megan turned in my arms, eyes heavily lidded, and

started giggling. "I'm not sure what I expected, but... holy shit. Mind blown."

"Same." I leaned in and kissed her cheek. "So, about that coffee...still up for that?"

"Oh yeah." She slowly detangled herself and helped me up. Her arms immediately went around me, hands squeezing my butt cheeks. "I'm going to need the energy."

"For...?"

"Round three, of course. Third time's the charm," she said, and tugged my face down to hers.

ACKNOWLEDGMENTS

My biggest thanks goes to my husband. I couldn't ask for a better cheerleader.

To the Red Reines—thank you for the critiques, advice, reality checks, and so much more. We make the tastiest sausage.

Thank you to Tobias Kashman, who did the sensitivity read for *Third Time's the Charm*. The story is better for it.

And to my readers, who make it all worthwhile.

Ryley Banks writes award-winning bestselling spicy romance, mostly of the LGBTQ+ variety. She's a connoisseur of tea and gin and loves language, especially creative profanity.

When she's not begging her characters to behave or reading fanfic, you can find Ryley watching cooking how-to videos, traveling, or, if you're lucky, crafting the next story to make you smile and set you on fire.

Stay up to date on all of Ryley's releases and more by subscribing to her VIP reader newsletter. Subscribers receive a free novelette, *Heat Waves*.

https://ryleybanks.com/ryleys-vip-newsletter/

Visit Ryley at: https://ryleybanks.com/

facebook.com/RyleyBAuthor

instagram.com/ryleybauthor

bookbub.com/authors/ryleybanks

goodreads.com/ryleybanks

Eggplant Night

Dirty Dishes

Teacher Pet

Third Time's the Charm

Anthologies

The Big Book of Orgasms Volume 2: 69 Sexy Stories
(featuring a shorter version of *Third Time's the Charm*)

Ink: Queer Sci Fi's Eighth Annual Flash Fiction Contest
(featuring *Right Place, Right Time*)

Nonfiction

Demystifying the Beats: How to Write a Killer Book by Carol
Potenza, Jordyn Kross, Ryley Banks, and Erin Krueger

HEAT WAVES

A Spicy MM Kraken
Shifter Monster Romance

*The king will have his elven mate in his arms again—
all eight of them—no matter the cost.*

Woodland elf Kalysin is thrust into a riptide of dreams as a dangerous drought parches the land. Stolen memories of a bronzed muscled figure who bathed him in ecstasy, but disappeared back into the sea, gone forever.

Could the dreams bubbling up from forgotten depths have anything to do with the shadowy stalker in the forests surrounding his liege's orchards and withering fields of crops? Or have they been stirred up by an evil magic that threatens famine and starvation across the lands? When Kal is forced to make a sacrifice to save his mother, will he survive long enough to be reclaimed by his mate? Or will the real monster doom him to take his memories to the grave?

Keep reading for an exclusive excerpt from *Heat Waves*, now available for free!

Excerpt from Heat Waves

The elf's whisper-quiet steps should have kept him well hidden. And they would—but not from me. His long brown hair was swept back and tied out of his way. My mouth watered. What if I gave in to the urge to sink my pointed canines into his neck, dragging them down the flesh to hear him cry out? My body tensed, eager to take take *take*. No. It wasn't time. But soon, he'd remember he belonged to me.

———

"Did you see that?" I froze, my long fingers stretched toward a low hanging bunch of nectar fruit. I gestured with my chin. "Over there."

Vulen, my assistant, turned his gaze toward the tree line. Nothing moved, though I was certain I'd seen an unnatural shadow. "I'm sorry, Kalysin. I must have missed it." His gray eyes swept back to me. "Perhaps you should have a drink of water. It's been so hot and dry—"

"I'm fine"—*absolutely not hallucinating, or insane, or seeing things*—"unlike these nectar fruit. They should be smooth, shiny. A vibrant green. But this whole orchard is sickly." I touched the cluster of fruit, and half of them dropped to the ground, joining countless others. I picked up several and gave them to Vulen, who labeled and packed them away for inspection.

Lord Elmar had demanded I meet with him that morning about the crops. I'd rushed in late, meeting Vulen at the door. Lord Elmar had been in his conservatory.

"What am I giving you coin for, Kalysin, as my Overseer of Lands, if you don't actually *oversee*?" He clenched a freshly picked furry yellow fruit in his hand so hard the fruit's skin began to split, separating from the flesh. "Consequences, Kalysin, and dire ones, if this continues—your tardiness and the deteriorating harvest. You should be able to do *something* since your own lands are producing. We all must make sacrifices."

He dropped the mangled fruit, and it hit the marble floor with a muffled wet thud. A servant swept in and cleaned up every trace.

I'd bowed in acquiescence, unwilling to brave Lord Elmar's reaction if I told him the reason I was late was because his messenger had notified me at an ungodly early hour, and I'd arrived as soon as I could.

As Vulen and I finished with the nectar fruit orchard, taking a few more samples, I panicked over what to tell Lord Elmar. What were samples of crops going to show, other than the simple fact the plants weren't getting enough water?

"We're going to the brambleberries next?" Vulen asked, adjusting his water packs.

"Yes." Lord Elmar had also made it clear our rate of crop monitoring was unsatisfactory. "I don't want another meeting like this morning's if we can help it."

"I was afraid he would strike you," Vulen whispered as we made our way across Lord Elmar's vast lands to the next planted plot, our sandaled feet kicking up a plume of dust behind us as though the ground didn't remember what it was like to be wet.

"Me too," I admitted. "But it's no matter. I'm fortunate Lord Elmar gave me a position other than as a servant or messenger." Or so I kept reminding myself.

The brambleberry bushes were planted in interminably long tracts. We settled under a scrubby tree that provided some shade about halfway down one of the lines. Vulen removed the packs he carried and wiped the sweat from his forehead. I drank from my water-skin, half empty already. I swallowed, then knelt in the sandy dirt, peering under the lowest brambleberry branches. A concerning number of hard, green-white fruit. After carefully plucking two of the few ripe black ones, I offered Vulen one and popped the other in my mouth. The sweet, tangy juice rushed over my tongue, and I closed my eyes, taking brief joy in one of the few perks of my work. I hummed, transported back to my time as a youngling, raiding my mother's brambleberry bushes with— My brows knit together. I couldn't recall my playmate's features, much less their name.

But the headache I had from the effort to remember was very real indeed. They'd been happening increasingly often, as were the dreams slipping through my mind like a handful of seawater as soon as I woke each morning.

"Are you well, Kalysin?" Vulen asked, his head tilted to the side.

"No. This damned heat." I spit out a seed that had lodged in my teeth. "Let's get this over with."

We trudged onward, the top branches of the long, staked rows of thorny bushes repeating the same story as the lower ones with the addition of curled, sun-scorched leaves.

"Do you remember when it last rained?" I asked Vulen.

He frowned. "I—maybe late spring? Or perhaps it was early spring." Vulen stared off in the distance, over the rolling hills and the cloudless blue sky.

"I can't remember either," I admitted. The rains had not come this summer to fill the streams and rivers to bursting like they had in the past, yet I'd held out hope the drought hadn't affected the crops. Between the brambleberries, the nectar fruit earlier, and the sickly patches of spike melons we'd inspected before them, this was nothing like I'd ever seen.

The midday summer sun burned my tanned arms, but my skin prickled as though a winter chill had blown in. Someone was watching me.

Not us.

Me.

Continue reading *Heat Waves* by Ryley Banks, available for free on BookFunnel.

Copyright © 2023 by Ryley Banks

SACKED BY THE QUARTERBACK

A MM Enemies to
Lovers Sports Romance

The Locker Room Playbooks Book 1

When you play for the same team, there's a fine line between love and hate.

As the MVP on the university football team, Paul Martell doesn't get distracted. Ever.

Not even by quarterback Will MacLeod in the locker room shower.

But after an epic fumble during their big homecoming game almost spells disaster, can a Hail Mary recover their chance to be together?

Keep reading for an exclusive excerpt from *Sacked by the Quarterback*, available now wherever books are sold!

Excerpt from Sacked by the Quarterback

I shoved myself into the huddle with the rest of the offense, breath steaming from under our face masks in the cold October air. My lungs burned as I sucked in oxygen, but my cheeks flamed in disgrace.

"Clock's running out and we're only down by seven points, so we've gotta make a move." Quarterback Will MacLeod jabbed a gloved finger at the other wide receiver then turned to me. "Martell, the ball's coming to you *if* you can get out in front of your defender. They won't expect it after you couldn't get your hands on the last one. Think you can take what I give you? 'Cause it's coming hard." He gave me a cocked-eyebrow grin with that fucking awful double-entendre challenge.

I ground my teeth so violently they creaked as the rest of the offense in the huddle whooped over the screaming crowd, fake-scandalized. But the desperation that had haunted the offensive line since late in the third quarter finally broke.

Not that I'd tell him, but MacLeod's plan was a good move, especially for a second string QB and a walk-on. And it'd give me a chance to redeem myself after I'd fucked up, starting too late down the field and barely touching the ball as I failed to catch his pass.

That asshole was on his knees in front of us—how many times had I pictured him in this exact position? So I crowded over him until he looked up. My blood thundered with testosterone as we stared at each other.

"Anything you give me, I can handle," I replied. The huddle erupted with laughter again. I bared my teeth and shoved my mouth guard back in.

MacLeod's green eyes flashed. "You'd better, Martell," he said around a too-cocky grin. "Or your ass is mine."

My face burned for an entirely different reason.

The huddle broke and I lined up wide right. Everything depended on this catch—State U winning the homecoming game against our conference rivals, for one. Securing my athletic scholarship for another year.

Giving my parents bragging rights at the next family get-together. And, oh yeah, whether ESPN's talking heads would later be babbling about "junior wide receiver Paul Martell's butter fingers" or "Martell's impossible game-winning catch."

Little would they know that my mistake earlier had less to do with my skills and more to do with the epic distraction that was Will *motherfucking* MacLeod.

My world narrowed to the game. The ball snapped. I sprinted toward the endzone. Eight yards down, I angled across the field, losing the defender chasing me entirely. I whipped my head to MacLeod.

Damn. He'd done it. The pass was fucking perfect. Released just as he got pummeled into the turf.

I leaped, vaulting over an opposing player who dropped low to take out my knees.

My hands locked around the football, and I cradled it into my body. Secure. It *had* to be.

I slammed into the ground, breath punched out of me—

Continue reading *Sacked by the Quarterback* by Ryley Banks, available wherever books are sold.

9 781962 835107